cl✿verleaf books™

Off to School

3 1526 05032114 7

Sofia's First Day of School

by **Lisa Bullard**

Illustrated by **Miki Sakamoto**

Ⅶ MILLBROOK PRESS • MINNEAPOLIS

For Mrs. Henriques, the teacher
who made every day of school
such a pleasure!—L.B.

To my high school teacher Mr.
Gill, who inspired me to keep
creating!—M.S.

Text and illustrations copyright © 2018 by
Lerner Publishing Group, Inc.

Millbrook Press
A division of Lerner Publishing Group, Inc.
241 First Avenue North
Minneapolis, MN 55401 USA

For reading levels and more information, look up this title at
www.lernerbooks.com.

Main body text set in Slappy Inline 22/28.
Typeface provided by T26.

Library of Congress Cataloging-in-Publication Data

The Cataloging-in-Publication Data for *Sofia's First Day of School*
   is on file at the Library of Congress.
ISBN 978-1-5124-3936-6 (lib. bdg.)
ISBN 978-1-5124-5579-3 (pbk.)
ISBN 978-1-5124-5105-4 (EB pdf)

Manufactured in the United States of America
1-42149-25422-1/5/2017

TABLE OF CONTENTS

Chapter One

It's a Big Day!

I put on my school clothes, zip my pencils inside my backpack, and hug my dog, Roscoe.

"The first day of school is a big deal,"
I tell him. "And I'm so **excited!**"

5

Dad fixes pancakes for breakfast, but I'm not very hungry so I sneak some to Roscoe. Maybe I'm a little **nervous**.

Many people, even grown-ups, get nervous about new things.

6

Dad takes my picture before Mom and Roscoe walk me to the bus stop.

On the bus, Sadie from the park lets me sit with her. We talk all the way to school.

8

Chapter Two

My New Classroom

At school, a grown-up helps me find my classroom.

The grown-ups at school make students feel welcome.

I sit at a desk that has my name on it. When I open my backpack, I find a note that says, "We love you!"

The boy next to me looks **nervous** too, so I share my pencil sharpener with him.

Oliver

Sofia

13

Our teacher, Mrs. Hernandez, has a big, friendly smile. "We'll learn lots of fun things this year," she says.

There's a lot to remember the first day, but teachers remind students again on day two.

14

Then she tells us the school rules that keep everyone safe and happy.

Chapter Three

My New School

Some schools call their library the media center.

My class travels around the school together.

I can't wait to read all the books in the library!

I remember how to get my lunch in the lunchroom.

And I make a basket at recess!

At the end of the day, Sadie and I sit together on the bus again. We both had a **great** day!

Chapter Four

A Great First Day!

When I get home, Roscoe gives me a big kiss.

"School is fun, Roscoe," I say.

"And my stomach is all better, so no people food for you tonight!"

21

Frame It!

Many families celebrate the first day of school by taking a special photograph. Why not prepare for your next First Day of School photo by creating a special frame for it?

What You Will Need
a sheet of newspaper or
    paper towel
4 wooden craft sticks
glue
items to decorate your frame, such
    as markers, sequins, buttons,
    and stickers

1) Put the newspaper or paper towel on a table or desk to make your working surface.

2) Line up your 4 craft sticks on top of this in the shape of a square. You are going to glue the 4 sticks together into this square shape.

3) Start by putting a spot of glue at the bottom end of one of the craft sticks that will form the sides of the square. Form the first corner by gluing this end to the craft stick that will be the bottom of the square. Hold the two ends together for a short time to help the glue stick.

4) Continue to glue the rest of the sticks together, forming corners to finish the square.

5) Set the frame aside for a short time to allow the glue to dry.

6) Once the glue has fully dried, decorate your frame with colored markers or stickers or by gluing on colorful buttons, sequins, or other items.

GLOSSARY

excited: eager and interested

media center: a room or building that stores books, technology, and other resources

nervous: worried about something

pencil sharpener: a tool that shaves a pencil end to a sharp point

welcome: to make people feel that you are glad they are there

TO LEARN MORE

BOOKS

Benjamin, Tina. *My Day at School.* New York: Gareth Stevens, 2015.
Follow the photos and words in this book to learn about another student's school day.

Bullard, Lisa. *William's 100th Day of School.* Minneapolis: Millbrook Press, 2018.
Read this fun story about how William celebrates the 100th day of school.

Ruurs, Margriet. *School Days around the World.* Tonawanda, NY: Kids Can, 2015.
Read this book to learn what going to school is like for children in different countries around the world.

WEBSITES

Calendar Game
http://www.abcya.com/calendar_word_problems.htm
Play this game so that you can learn how to find your first day of school on a calendar.

School Jokes Pages
http://boymamateachermama.com/wp-content/uploads/2013/08/school-jokes-BMTM-PDF.pdf
Visit this page to solve some fun school riddles!

School Words
http://www.enchantedlearning.com/books/school/words
Put this book together, color the pages, and practice school words as you get ready for the first day of school!

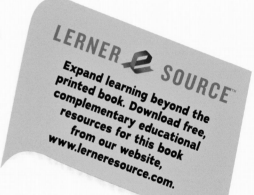

LERNER ⅇ SOURCE™
Expand learning beyond the printed book. Download free, complementary educational resources for this book from our website, www.lerneresource.com.

INDEX